Beginnings

Lenore Lang

To Bethany —
Thank you for your testimony today!
Lenore Lang

Scripture taken from the New King James Version. Copyright © 1982 by Thomas Nelson, Inc. Used by permission. All rights reserved.

ISBN 978-1-61225-078-6

Copyright © 2011 Lenore Lang
All Rights Reserved

No part of this publication may be reproduced in any form or stored, transmitted or recorded by any means without the written permission of the author.

Published by Mirror Publishing
Milwaukee, WI 53214
www.pagesofwonder.com

Printed in the USA

To my husband, George,
My beloved partner and encourager.
"We are a team."

Acknowledgments

To these who have helped bring this book to fruition:

Rita Weber, who listened as I read to her my manuscript, and who gave encouragement from page one to the end;

Patti Sisson, who put my steps on the path which eventually led to Milwaukee and Mirror Publishing;

Linda Lang Peterson, our daughter, the photographer of the picture on the front cover;

Neal Wooten, Manager and Publisher of his Pages of Wonder, Mirror Publishing.

To all, my deep gratitude.

- Lenore Lang

Foreword

It is an honor to write a few words for this beautiful book by Lenore Lang.

Beginnings is a powerful blend of ideas and well-crafted words unlike any I have read.

My friend and mentor first read through her manuscript for me while we sat in her sunroom where we meet for frequent Friday afternoon visits. On the day she asked permission to share her work, I smiled. Of course I would love to hear what she had written. She had shared many things over the years. Nothing prepared me for the story I was about to hear.

I had always loved the story of Adam and Eve in the Garden. It captivated me, as I thought about the wonder of living in the very presence of God in such a perfect place, and I had spent many hours contemplating the reality of their altered life after the fall – the grief, the struggles, and the tragic sense of separation they must have experienced.

Yet, Lenore took a more intimate look in her ponderings about those two and their day-to-day experiences, the evidences of life in a newly-fallen world, those evidences coloring every conversation, every encounter, every challenge. The pain of their loss became palpable to me and often brought tears to my eyes as I listened to her read.

Still, through all the chapters there was a dimension I had not considered – glimpses of the One who had made them, continued to love them, and who desired to be with them as much as they wanted and needed Him.

Such thoughts had not occurred to me before, along with the idea that if He could have continued as before, He would have, but it was not possible. The foreshadowing of events to come would provide a path of forgiveness and reconciliation. That path was there in the book of Genesis, but it was only clear in retrospect.

Beginnings brings inspired understanding of an all-loving God, revealing an unfulfilled human existence in the absence of communion with God and pointing us toward the hope of a return one day to a place of perfection in the Holy presence of the God who loves us with an everlasting love.

Enjoy the story. Allow yourself to step into the place of Adam or Eve. Let the Spirit guide you to the truths which are there for you to discover as you walk with those two, with the "knowledge of Good and Evil" stark realities for each of us as we walk the paths of this world.

- Rita J. Weber

CHAPTER 1

The sound awakened the man. A new sound, from the woman—soft snuffling noises. In the darkness he couldn't understand. He reached out his hand and touched her bare shoulder. It was wet, and trembled beneath his touch. A long sigh swept through him. Things were so different now. Strangely different.

The differences had begun when they walked out the garden gate. Not that they wanted to. He had given them no choice. Resistance? Useless. And they both knew it. They knew why. That other choice had settled the issue.

Before that, -- choices were wonderful. "Which fruit should we try today?" They were all so good..........

"Let's go bathe in the stream," he'd say, and they did, the water clear as crystal, cool and soothing on bare skin.

"Let's watch the monkeys! See how they climb up and down the trees – so fast!"

Another sound roused him from his memories. Louder this time. Yes, it was coming from Eve. He reached toward her. "Eve, what's wrong?" Why ask? He knew. It was the sadness again.

All too well he knew that sadness for himself. But maybe, just maybe, it would help to talk. Talk had been so good before. Free, without constraint or fear. And now, fear walked with them, between them, all the time.

The other walking – how could he forget? Those other walks had been wonderful – with Him in the cool of the day. They'd talk and laugh and listen in ways that he somehow knew would never come again. All these thoughts flashed through his mind in an instant.

"Oh Adam – you know. I can't stand it – knowing how things were – then – and how they are – now."

"I know. I feel the same."

"Do you – blame me?"

"Blame you for feeling this way?" It was double talk and he knew it the moment the words were out of his mouth. And why was he whispering? Who was there to hear? The One who walked with them – before – was gone. That's all. Gone.

The thought thudded against his heart and left a gaping sadness. A sadness that was tinged with another emotion – blame. That's why the double talk and he knew it. Did he blame her? Of course he did.

At the same time he blamed himself. Perhaps that was part of the problem. This woman, so much a part of him, was to blame but the blame came back on himself again and again.

"What else could I have done?" he thought dully. "He said we'd die if we ate. There she was alive, beautiful in front of me, holding out the fruit. I had thought – 'He's wrong. She ate – and did not die.' So I ate too."

And now -- Die. What did that mean anyway? The word had a hard sound, immutable and ugly. He thought to himself, "I still don't know what it means, do I?"

The meaning was all tangled up with the knowledge that he – they – had not obeyed Him. The One who looked like them, had walked with them, talked with them, laughed with them. He knew their thoughts and their hearts. He answered their questions. What wonderful things He had shown them in that beautiful Garden.

The best fruits.

Places to sleep, soft and grassy.

The delights of a sunrise, the wonder of a sunset.

The sounds of birds singing.

The antics of the animals.

Ah yes, those animals. What a time he and Eve had had with the animals, talking. Well, no, he reflected, not talk as the three of them talked, but – almost. He could look into the eyes of a lion and know what it wanted. There was an acuteness of understanding that he strained now to remember.

Because the understanding was broken now, after He killed one of the animals to make clothes for himself and Eve.

To die. Yes, in his heart he knew what it was. But – was it the same for the animals as for the two of them? The animal – living no longer. The coat of the animal – clothes for his body, for her body, to cover their nakedness.

Nakedness they had not even been aware of – before. Nakedness that they were acutely aware of now, so they covered themselves as best they could. He laughed bitterly as he remembered those first frantic efforts to put together large leaves to clothe themselves.

Suddenly his thoughts were interrupted by a loud cry. Eve again. Not a soft snuffling this time, but a loud and bitter cry. Now she was sitting up beside him, in the darkness. "Why don't you say something? Can't you tell I want to talk?" The words were accusing and hurtful and for a moment all he wanted was to give some right back, even more accusing and hurtful than hers.

But something restrained him. The knowledge that it would do no good. The understanding that He would not want that. Even now, he remembered something of the wonder of their talk together, before – that awful day.

"I was just thinking….."

"Don't think so much. Talk to me!" The words again – accusing and hurtful.

"I want to, Eve, but – what can we do? What can I say? That I'm sorry? Of course I am. You know that….."

"Yes, and I know that you blame me!"

There it was again, -- the blame. "We started doing that in the Garden, and we've never stopped, have we."

"In the Garden?"

"You know. I told Him that the woman He brought to me, gave me the fruit and I ate. What was that but blame?"

"You blamed Him!"

"Yes, of course I did."

"Why?"

"There you go – asking impossible questions. No wonder I can't talk with you anymore!"

"Adam, what are we going to do? How are we going to live – this way? We – we can't!"

"He said to go forth and multiply and fill up the earth."

"Fill up the earth. It's not good here like in the Garden. Can't we go back?"

He sighed bitterly. "You know we can't. That angel

of fire wouldn't let us. And besides, He wouldn't be there with us, not in the same way."

"The same way. I wish things were the same again."

"They won't be. They can't be. You know that. I know that."

"I know that I felt – loved, there in the Garden, Adam. It was beautiful. We had so much there."

"Well, we still have plants and trees and flowers, here, don't we?"

"Yes, but – Oh, it seems to take so much longer to get food to eat. And some of the fruit trees are missing, you know, the ones He showed us. He told us what they were for, and He told us they would be good for us. Now, some of them – we don't find them anymore, do we."

"One was the Tree of Life, He said. Isn't that what He said? And that's one of the reasons that we had to leave the Garden, remember? He didn't want us eating that fruit any more, and 'living forever' is the way He put it."

"Would we have lived forever, Adam?"

"I think so."

"And now?"

"No."

"But what is forever? What does it mean to – die?"

"That's what I've been thinking about when I heard you crying."

"Why didn't you say so?"

"How could I?"

"How could you not? I can't read your mind."

Anger flared within him. "I didn't think you'd understand."

"I understand more than you think. Why can't you believe that?"

"Because – oh, I don't know why I feel this division between us now. It was never there before."

"Before I ate the fruit. I know what you're trying to say. The blame again."

"Eve, we can't go on this way. We've got to work together, the way we used to do."

A long sigh from Eve's lips ruffled her hair and she pushed it back from her forehead before she lay back down beside Adam in the darkness which enveloped them. Not a comforting kind of darkness, but a fear-filled void that caused her to creep close to him, in a vain effort to ease her own heart's cry.

He reached for her and the former yearnings and closeness and ecstasy came rushing in. For a while it was wonderful, as it had been before -- almost, but not quite the same. Eve sensed it too. But finally, entwined in each others arms, they fell asleep.

CHAPTER 2

They did not stray far from the Garden. Somehow it felt better to be near, even though the presence of the fiery angel always blocked the entrance.

Often in the evenings they walked past the Eastern Gate. That was where He had given them the clothing after the killing of the lamb. Adam remembered the remorse in His eyes, the indefinable sadness. Something in his soul had wanted to cry out, "No, don't do it! Don't kill that lamb!" but some other sense restrained him.

Now they were able to gain some sense of closeness to Him at that place, and they began to realize that it was pleasing to Him when they offered a sacrifice. So that is what they did, and each time it helped them to remember how it had been when the three of them walked together. Sometimes they caught a glimpse of Him on the other side of the gate, looking at them, always with a sadness in His eyes. Sadness that twisted their hearts and brought bitter reproach again and again to fill their days.

But those days were harder now, and sometimes as Adam worked in the fields, trying to find food for them to eat, he would remember those words: 'In the sweat of your face you shall eat bread,' and each time the anger, the remorse, the fear would well up inside of him again. (Genesis 3:19)

Besides, it wasn't just for the two of them that he had to find bread now. Soon, there would be another. He had watched, almost in awe, as day after day Eve's belly had grown a little larger. At first, imperceptibly, and they both hardly knew what was happening. Then, the knowledge could not be denied. Soon there would be another one of them.

They both understood that it was in those precious moments of closeness that it had happened. Oh, they had observed their animal friends in their mating rituals. Adam shook his head ruefully when he found himself thinking "animal friends," because he still thought of them that way, from the days in the Garden.

But he and Eve had also realized that for themselves, this growing of another being like themselves was different from the animals. The animals could bear young in not much time at all, some of them.

But for themselves, this process was longer, much longer. He looked up from his work and saw Eve walking toward him, graceful even with the added weight that stuck out in front of her like a rounded melon. "How beautiful she is!" he said to himself. "Even with all we've gone through, she is bone of my bone, flesh of my flesh, and Yes, I love her. He was good to give her to me. If only......"

He could not go on with the thought. What had happened, had happened. It was now important for them to go on with what was left. Shut out from the Garden, they would just have to go on.

"What are you thinking about, my Adam?"

The question no longer surprised him. She asked it so often that it had lost its edge and the power to disturb him. Most of the time, anyway. When he was tired or worn out from the constant work it was another story. Sharp words came easily then, words he often regretted until it was too late.

Regrets aside now, he smiled, tenderness washing through him, and seeing his smile, Eve said to herself, "He is so handsome! I'm glad He brought me to him. I'm bone of his very bone. Will this one inside me feel that too?"

"One of these days, we will know what it's like to have another one like us!"

"Oh, Adam, do you think it will be – hard?"

"Hard? Well, I don't know. I think we will just have to see how it goes, having a baby with us."

"No, no, Adam, I don't mean – that! Don't you know what I mean?"

Adam groaned inwardly. "There she goes again, expecting me to know what she means when she might not even know herself!" But out loud he said, as calmly as he could, as calmly as he had learned from bitter experience, "Tell me."

"You know…..He said, 'I will greatly multiply your sorrow and your conception. In pain you shall bring forth children'….(Genesis 3:16) That's the part I worry about, Adam…. in pain! Don't you see?"

"Yes, " Adam thought ruefully, "I do see and I've thought about that part, even though I don't want to think about it." Aloud, he said, "Yes, Eve, I see. All I know is, -- surely He will help you through it."

"Help me through it? Maybe I don't want to go through it. I…..I'm afraid, Adam."

He walked over to her, and putting his arm around her slim shoulders, he drew her to him. "I know. Yes, sometimes, I'm afraid, too. But -- I'll be here for you. I'll do what I can to make it easier."

"Then it will be hard."

"Did I say that?"

"You said you'd do what you can to make it easier. That means easier than – it would be otherwise. That means -- hard."

The frustration welled up in his heart again. What she said made sense, and he knew it. It seemed she was always doing that, tricking him with words. But all he answered was, "Yes. Yes, it will be hard."

"But – you'll be here. You won't leave me, Adam?"

"Of course not. We're in this together now. I'll do my best."

CHAPTER 3

And he did do his best. The day that they both dreaded came at last. The contractions were easy at first, he noticed. But then – harder and harder. Eve was brave, and his own heart was torn as he saw unmistakably the pain that took hold of her as she waited and panted and pushed.

Afterward, as he held his newly-born son, he looked over at Eve and saw an indefinable look in her eyes, -- defiance and relief and something else he couldn't quite read. She lay there watching the two of them, and then reached out her arms to enfold their child.

It was then that she said the words: "I have gotten a man from the Lord." (Genesis 4:1)   Ah. That was what she had been thinking.

His own heart echoed the words and he nodded. "Yes. Yes, and I tried to help you through it, Eve.   Was it – was it as hard as you thought?"

She pushed back a strand of damp hair from her cheek, and mused, "Well, I really had no idea of what it would be like. I've watched the animals give birth, and I've wondered about the pain."

"The pain,-- it must have been bad."

"Not easy. But – now it's over. I'm glad. Yes, I have gotten a man from the Lord. He did help. Don't you think He knows, Adam?"

"Of course He does. Perhaps soon – we'll take a sacrifice to the Eastern Gate and let Him know how thankful we are."

So they did, as soon as Eve felt strong enough. She carried their small son gently, and Adam brought the lamb for the sacrifice. "What shall we call him, this first son?"

"Any ideas?"

"Yes, -- Cain, Adam. Let's call him Cain."

What joy that child brought to them. Each day they watched, stroked his small head, looked for the light of recognition in his eyes. He drank hungrily from Eve's breasts, and the milk agreed with him, because he grew almost before their eyes. Eve learned to carry him in a small sling on her hip, doing chores that she could, to help Adam.

Often they were tired at the end of the day, and sometimes they thought longingly of those walks with Him.

In those days, they hadn't even known the word "tired". But now it was a different story. The days were long and hard. Food was plentiful and grew well in the soil, but it seemed that it took a lot of effort to cultivate it and to keep the weeds from taking over.

Adam thought sometimes about His words back in the Garden: "tend and keep it" (Genesis 2:15) and he had done just that, but the work was full of joy then. It had seemed easy. His forehead had never been drenched with sweat then. But now – always.

One night, as tired as he was, he couldn't sleep. Just as he would doze off, he'd hear a sound and would jerk awake, listening. He looked over at Eve, cradling the baby in her arms as she slept. He remembered something, -- the feeling of drowsiness that had come over him the day He had performed the operation that brought Eve to him.

It had been surprising, really. He had awakened and had seen her for the first time. In all the days of looking at the animals, carefully choosing names for them, he had experienced joy in the process. Exhilaration! A feeling of accomplishment, and of gratitude to Him for the chance to use his mind in such a way.

But -- that other day had been different. He thought again of the rapture that had filled him when he looked at this creature who lay beside him when he awoke that first time and saw her. Her beauty…..he caught his breath when he remembered.She had looked at him, in return, and had smiled. Their eyes caught and held. He had reached out a hand to take her own, and their fingers had gently intertwined.

And then – ah, He had said the words that bound them to each other. "It is not good for you to be alone, Adam. I have made a helpmate for you. Taken from you. Take care of her. Together you will work in the Garden." (Genesis 2:18) And they did.

Day after day, their love for each other had grown. "She is bone of my bones, flesh of my flesh. I will call her – Woman, for she was taken out of me, out of myself as a Man." (Genesis 2:23)

His breathing came out in a sigh as he remembered. Eve stirred in her sleep beside him and the child beside her whimpered. Adam lay still until he heard again their quiet breathing. Finally, he also fell asleep, but it was a sleep troubled by wild dreams. Again he was standing in the Garden, under that tree. Again the fruit was in his hand, but this time he threw it, high, high, into the sky, hearing mocking laughter as it fell to earth with a thud.

CHAPTER 4

When he awoke with the morning light, his head was aching, his mind distracted with the remembrance of a restless night. Eve, too, seemed restless and remote, her attention occupied with keeping Cain happy and contented. Adam felt small stirrings that he could not quite explain.

Why should she spend so much time with this child? Well, yes, our child, he mused. At the same time as these jealous thoughts came, almost unbidden, to his mind, he knew they were wrong but was powerless to stop them. Only backbreaking work in the fields kept his mind diverted for a time from thinking the thoughts he hated at the same time that he clung to them.

How different it had been, -- before. Sometimes the regrets threatened to smother him. He sensed that Eve felt the same, because sometimes he caught her gaze upon him when he turned to look at her out of the corner of his eye. Her eyes held – what? Feelings that he could not fathom. Hate? Anger? Disgust? Remorse?

Yes, all that, and more. Yet he knew that there were times she clung to him, almost in desperation, willing away the bad thoughts that came. And still he loved her. He knew she loved him, too. Almost as before, but – no, not the same. Before – the love was free and easily given, with no hindrances.

Now, conflicts flickered at the edges of their relationship, eager to flare up at the least provocation. He could sense it. And at those times, he remembered again the tree: the Tree of the Knowledge of Good and Evil. (Genesis 2:17) The serpent had lied. Well, actually he had spoken the truth – to a point. But along with the truth, he had left out an important part.

"They would know," he had said. (Genesis 3:5) And indeed they did. They now had the knowledge of good and evil, but – what the serpent had not said was that they would no longer be innocent of evil, and beyond that, would be powerless to withstand it.

Adam yearned for those days of innocence. His heartache colored all he did, all he said, and sometimes erupted into anger out of sheer frustration. At those times he hacked away furiously at the weeds that threatened to choke the good grain he was trying to cultivate on his farm. The very act of pounding the ground gave him a little relief.

And what was the other thing the serpent had said. Eve had reported the conversation to him in the moments after they had eaten the fruit, the forbidden fruit. She had ventured the story hesitantly: "When I told him that He said we must not eat it or we will die, he said, 'Oh no, you will not die! You'll be like Him, knowing good and evil.'" (Genesis 3:4-5)

"And you believed him? Why?"

"He seemed so reasonable and it sounded so right, Adam! Besides, I always did wonder what that fruit would taste like! Didn't you? Remember, we talked about it."

Adam had to admit she was correct. They had talked about it, but he had always told her patiently what He had said.

And Eve had interjected: "When the – the serpent said we would be wise – like Him –well, it seemed such a great thing. Wasn't He wise, always, my Adam?"

Adam had to agree. "Yes, -- yes, of course He was, -- He Is, -- and yes, I know what you mean. To be wise like He is, yes, that would be wonderful."

"But we aren't, now, are we." It was more of a statement than a question. And his own heart had echoed the thought.

To be wise like He is -- ah, no. What a goal, -- but

he laughed bitterly, remembering. He knew now how impossible it was, for him, and for her. To know what to do, to know the good, -- that was one thing. But to have even the desire to really do it. He had to admit it wasn't in him, not the way it had been – before.

All of these thoughts swirled through his mind during his waking hours, hours spent wresting food from unforgiving ground. And that was what He had said: "In the sweat of your face you shall eat bread." (Genesis 3:19) It was a struggle, a never-ending struggle.

He tried again to remember the lightness of heart that had been theirs. It eluded him. Made a mockery of him. Oh yes. Sometimes they laughed together, especially at the antics of their small son, Cain. They would watch him as he tried to crawl through the grass, inching along, making small grunting noises.

They would look at each other. One day Eve voiced his own wonderings: "You and I – we never had to do that, did we?"

"No—we were just – just grown up when He made us, weren't we! We didn't have to learn all that." And, he reflected to himself, we didn't have any parents around to watch us grow, not like we are doing with this small one. But he understood that the process had to start somewhere. He remembered the joy he and Eve had shared in learning together from Him. To be that wise, to know good – and its opposite, evil, and yet not to be a slave to that evil………..

He shook his head to clear the fog in his thoughts. It was too much. He'd never master it. How could he? What was ahead for him, for her, for this child? He wished he knew.

CHAPTER 5

The days wore on, one after the other. Now they had the distraction of a son to watch. His insistent attempts to crawl had escalated into walking, -- first, stumbling footsteps, then more assured attempts to follow his father and mother wherever they went. He seemed to like best to walk the furrows behind his father, and often Adam would hear his frustrated babbling as he tried to keep up.

Each time, Adam would stop, and pick up his small son, and together they would view the growing grain and plants. It pleased Adam that Cain was so interested, and he knew that Eve was glad when he spent time with their son. She was again heavy with a second pregnancy and appreciated his help in corralling an often willful and stubborn little boy.

Sometimes a vague sense of foreboding gripped

Adam as he tried to deal with his son, but he would shake it off and often ended up laughing at the antics of this, his firstborn. And Cain blossomed in the approval of his father. Often he would put back his little head and laugh along with Adam. A special bond grew between them, and Adam was glad that He had blessed them with this son.

This feeling of closeness was marred at times by Cain's playfulness with the sheep that Adam had shepherded into an enclosure. He would take up a stone and fling it, helter-skelter toward the animals as they grazed nearby. Adam still retained a sense of the camaraderie he and Eve had had with the animals in the Garden, and it hurt him in an indefinable sort of way when he saw this behavior. Yet he held back from saying anything.

Once in a while, he would go to Cain, grip his small hand and gently lead him back to the garden he had been cultivating, hoping thus to turn away Cain from destructive behavior. At those time he would wonder to himself how to deal with his son. "We didn't learn any of that when we were – young," he'd say to Eve, and she would nod in agreement.

"We'll just have to do the best we can," she'd say.

Nearly ready for birth again, Eve seemed distracted, and Adam remembered how it had been just before Cain was born.

He tried to bring up the subject again, but for the

most part was met with stoic silence. "I'll try to be there for you – again, Eve," he'd say. She would gaze at him with a look in her eyes he could not read, then sigh and go on with her work.

The work of getting food for the three of them seemed to sap all their energy. At times Eve would put down the stone she used to pound the grain, and would bury her head in her hands. The remembrance of the Garden where they had lived was strong at those times, but at the same time she was repelled by the memories. It seemed so pointless to have to do all this work, this bone-tiring work, for – what? Just to live? What had He told Adam? "In the sweat of your face you shall eat bread." (Genesis 3:19)

Eve would shake her head derisively and think, "And my face too." But the blame she sometimes felt toward Adam would invariably sink back onto herself, and then, almost in a fury, she would pick up the stone and pound the grain as if she could pound her thoughts to pieces. Only it never worked. The thoughts would come again and again, unbidden and unwelcome.

One day she said to Adam, "I wonder how it will be, having another child, another son."

Adam smiled at her, thinking again as he did so often, "My beautiful wife! My Eve….the mother of all living." (Genesis 3:20) Yes, he knew there would be more children and part of him welcomed the thought, but at the same time he was afraid.

But to Eve he said gently, "Well, how do you know this one will be a son, my Eve?"

She puckered her lips and a frown creased her forehead. "I just – I just know," and she tossed back her hair with a slim hand. He noticed the soil on her fingers, from the pounding stone that lay beside her on the ground. "Another son. How will that be? Have you wondered too?"

"Yes, yes, of course I have. I suppose," and here he stopped to think……"I suppose Cain won't know what to think, having a – a brother."

They both turned to look at their small son, asleep nearby on a soft lambskin. "He's precious, isn't he, Adam!" Eve's voice was soft, caressing.

"Yes, -- a precious gift from Him," agreed her husband.

And the days went by until again they knew the time had come for the new one to be born. Adam had made an enclosure for them, and it was in one of the rooms that again she labored and finally brought to birth their second son.

"Yes," thought Adam, "Eve was right. Another son."

Cain was asleep in an adjoining room when the event took place, and after he had washed his new child and was sure Eve was resting after her ordeal, he brought the baby to Cain. Hardly knowing what to say, he reached out and grasped Cain's small hand, then helped him stroke his brother's arm.

But Cain jerked away his hand impulsively, then began to run away. "No!"

It was a cry of – what? Adam was appalled. Anger? Frustration? He did not know. But something in his heart contracted in fear. Taking the baby back to Eve, he reached out his hand and said to Cain, "Come! We'll go for a walk!"

As they walked, Adam tried to talk to Cain about the baby. Abel. That was the name Eve had chosen. "You have a brother, Cain. His name is Abel."

Again, the word shot out of small Cain's mouth. "No!"

And again Adam was shocked to the depths of his soul. Nowhere in his mind did he have any idea of how to deal with this – this rebellion.But at the same time as that thought came, another shot forth and he knew, yes, he knew that this rebellion had begun with him, and with Eve. What else was it other than rebellion to turn away from Him and His gentle directives for their lives?

They had said No to Him, and now they would spend the rest of their lives – how long would that be? – in paying for that simple act of rebellion.Simple? No, he knew it was far from simple, an act that would complicate their lives – forever.

CHAPTER 6

The days piled up, one upon another. He kept a record on a clay tablet similar to the ones he had used for recording the names of the animals back in the Garden. Sunset, sunrise. Sunset, sunrise. Some days he was so weary he could hardly see, but he forced his mind to concentrate and count. It seemed important, why he could not say.

He dug the clay from a riverbank not far away and often marveled how easily it took the marks he made with a sharpened stick. But after a day or two in the sun, the impressions were there to stay. At first he tried to remember the names of the animals he had written – so long ago, it seemed. He had taught him how to do it, and somehow in the very act of recalling those words, Adam felt closer to Him. So not long after they left the Garden, he had started this task.

He tried to remember other thoughts that He had told them both: How in the beginning He had made the earth. Day by day. Sometimes he had to sit quietly for long moments at a time before the ideas would come back to him. Then he would remember and make the marks before the thought faded.

Finding him doing this one day, Eve asked, "What are you doing, my Adam?" And he tried to explain, to show her how to form the letters to make the words. She would watch and try, sometimes succeeding, sometimes throwing the stick down in disgust.

"Why? Why do this? Don't you have enough to do without this?"

Then he would nod slowly and put the clay tablets away for awhile, until later when he was drawn to them, again and again. If Eve found him working away again, he tried to explain. "I feel closer – closer to Him when I do this, Eve."

Her expression at those times was inscrutable. He could not tell if she was pleased or angry.But a wistful look would sometimes steal over her face and he knew she was remembering, too.

Remembering how it was in those days before the – how could he describe it? -- before their fall. It was a fall, he knew that now, a fall from the heights of pleasure and joy and communion with the One who knew them heart and soul, the One who had made them, had told them so many things.

Again his mind went to the writing. Forming the characters, trying to remember each one that He had taught him, back there in the Garden, back even before Eve came into his life. He had found great pleasure in the learning. And naming the animals as He brought them to him, ah, how wonderful that had been!

The animals. Some were still near them. Some were not, and in that he found a measure of safety, because the sense of peace and security they had had in the Garden was gone. In its place was fear.

It was the fear that had prompted him to build enclosures for the sheep so they could not wander off and get lost or scattered. And their own house? He had found stones and fashioned rooms so that they would be safe. He had made rafters from straight tree branches, and over them he spread leaves and dry grass. Before that, they had often found their skin and coverings wet with the heavy dew which covered them each morning. The morning mists seemed easier to deal with once they were inside their enclosure and they felt more secure, especially after Cain was born.

Their small son grew lithe and strong, still liking to follow his father as he went about the duties of planting, weeding, and later, harvesting. Adam was pleased with the delight that Cain found in these activities and looked forward to Abel's joining them when his footsteps became more sure. To his surprise, Abel was more interested in watching the sheep in their pens. He would spend long moments looking at them and was surprisingly at home among them.

He and Eve talked about the difference between their two sons.

"Why do you suppose that is?" asked Eve one evening as they sat watching the sunset. They had finished their evening meal and were watching the boys play together in the clearing in front of their house.

"I don't know, I'm sure," Adam answered. "It's -- it's just the way they are, I suppose. Which do you like best?"

"Which son?" she parried.

"Well, yes, I suppose that's what I meant," and Adam brushed his hair back with an impatient hand. "I," and his answer was almost defiant, "I think I like Cain because he follows me when I plant and work the garden."

"And I like Abel because he, well, he likes to be around the animals. Especially the lambs." Eve's answer had a pensive sound and Adam turned quickly to look into her eyes.

"Remember, it was a lamb that……" His words were broken off by her sobs. They had come so quickly that he was taken aback. Her shoulders shook as he held her in his arms, trying to comfort her.

But she shook him off quickly, saying abruptly, "It'll never be the same. Never. Adam, life is ……………"

"Life is hard now. I know." His hands trembled as he sat, lacing his fingers in and out, then rubbing them together in frustration.

"Hard? Hah! You aren't the one who has to bear the pain of child birthing, Adam. It's really hard! You'll never know!"

Words of anger and sharp retort were on his lips. "I've told you that I'd be there……." He pinched his lips together to stop the hurtful torrent. Inwardly he groaned and his thoughts reached out in desperation – to Him. "Help me, oh help me." He tried to picture how He had looked in the Garden, the laughter that had flowed between the three of them.

Suddenly Eve stood and reached out a hand to Adam, running her other hand over a face still wet with tears. "Come, let's walk together. Maybe we can remember how good that walking used to be, with Him." Her words were wistful now, the biting anger gone as quickly as it had come.

He stood and took her outstretched hand and together they made their way toward the grassy knoll where Cain and Abel played.

CHAPTER 7

And so it went, day by day, some days more tranquil than others. It seemed to Adam that the less they talked about how it had been – before – the better off they were. At least there weren't the bitter battles between them, the anger and blame. By accepting their lives as they were, they found a measure of peace, only occasionally allowing thoughts of what they remembered as their "other life" to surface in their conversations.

Yet together they often brought an offering to the Eastern Gate of the Garden, a kind of unspoken agreement that this was what they both wanted, a way of keeping in contact with the One who had been so central in their lives, before.

Sometimes they would catch a glimpse of Him through the smoke from the fire that consumed the lamb on the altar of stones which Adam had built, and their hearts would be torn again and yet strangely calmed by the knowledge that He was there waiting for them.

As time passed, marked by Adam on his store of clay tablets, their small sons were growing and maturing, and they too joined Adam and Eve in these sacrificial offerings. Adam knew that for his sons, the ritual could not hold the same significance as it did for himself and Eve, but he tried to explain.

"We – your mother and I – lived here in a beautiful Garden where many trees grew. Lots of different fruit trees. Life was easy. We had many animal friends."

Abel questioned: "What kind of animals?"

"Oh, many different kinds. Large and small. Elephants. Tigers. Chickens. Ducks. Sheep. Lambs. I named them all."

A laugh from Cain. "You named them all?"

"Why not? The One who put us there in the Garden brought them to me and asked me to do it."

"Why?"

"Don't you have a name?"

"Yes, of course. But – they're only animals."

Anger flared in Adam. "Only animals? But – He made them! They were our friends."

"Friends?"

Abel found himself defending his father's words.

"Yes, friends, -- I can understand that. I like the animals. They're my friends."

Cain was scornful. "I'd rather throw stones at them." He glanced slyly at his father, whose brow was puckered in a frown.

Adam was remembering the frustration he had felt when Cain first started the stone-throwing. He felt helpless to know what to say to his elder son. Almost roughly he changed the subject. "Your mother and I had a good life, there, with the animals and the plants and the trees. We enjoyed it and often He would come walk with us in the evenings, in the cool of the day."

It was Abel's turn to be perplexed. "Why are we here now, and – not there?"

Eve placed a hand on Abel's shoulder. "We disobeyed the One who put us there."

"What does that mean?" Cain's question was insistent and harsh.

"We took some fruit from one special tree, and – we shouldn't have done that." Her voice trembled with intensity. Adam put his arm around her waist, which had expanded again in the process of another child to come.

"So He sent you out of the Garden for that?" Cain was obviously unimpressed.

Adam's words were almost an echo of the question. "Yes, He sent us out of the Garden for that."

"Well, I don't think He was being very fair!" The outburst caught Adam by surprise.

"Yes, son, He was very fair. He told us what to do. He told us what not to do. And we did it anyway."

"Why?"

Adam looked at Eve and was surprised to see her beginning to laugh. She said, "Oh, you're so full of questions. That's enough for now. No more." And she gave Cain's arm a little push. You and Abel can run back to our house and see who gets there first," and the two began to run, fleet of foot, with their laughter singing through the evening breeze, solemn talk and questions forgotten.

Eve put her arm through Adam's and together they followed their sons. "You surprised me there," and he gently pushed back her hair from her eyes.

"That's the best I could do," and her voice was wistful. She added softly, "Sometimes laughing is the only way I can stand the thought of what we've lost."

CHAPTER 8

The third child Eve bore was a girl. When the birthing process was finished, Eve smiled up at Adam with a wistful look in her eyes. "One like me!" she whispered softly.

Adam smiled back. "I hope she will be just like you," and his finger traced the soft curve of the small lips and the diminutive nose.

"I've been hoping this one would be – female, Adam."

"Why? Aren't sons good enough?"

"It has nothing to do with being good enough. I was just – oh, just ready to have another woman around." And she smiled into Adam's eyes. "After all, there are three of you against one of me, but now, two of me. Isn't that a good thing?"

Adam had to agree. "Yes, it's a good thing. That's

what He told me when He brought you to me the very first time. How well I remember that day, Eve."

"Tell me."

So patiently Adam told the story to her eager ears, while she nursed their newest child. "It was wonderful to know He made you for me. He knew I needed you. He knows it still."

"Do you think so?"

"Of course He does."

"Do you think He knew……………what we would do?"

"You mean – that day in the Garden?"

"Yes, of course, what else?"

Anger rose in Adam's mind and in his eyes, which he kept downcast so Eve would not see. "I'm not sure, but – Yes, He probably did," and the words tasted bitter in his mouth.

Eve laid the child to one side and raised up on one elbow. "You hate me for that." The words were matter-of-fact and toneless.

"Hate you?" He asked the question, knowing she would want an answer, an answer he found it hard to give, because he hardly knew himself. He raised his head and looked into her eyes which were boring into his. He reached out his hand for hers and was reassured that she did not draw back. Still he hesitated. And then, "No, if there's anyone I hate, it's myself." There, it was out. Enough of the blame game. And what would she say to that now?

She closed her eyes, and he wondered what she was thinking. He was surprised to see a tear roll down her cheek, followed by more. She sat up, covering her face with her hands and sobs tore at her throat. As Adam watched, then reached for her to enfold her in his arms, he almost wished she could say words, any words, rather than endure the wrenching awfulness of the self-hate in her heart.

"I just wonder how we can go on like this. How can we help our children when we hardly know what to do about……." She caught her breath, then went on in a rush…. "about what we did. We can tell them the story, but will they understand? Really understand? I don't think so. You heard what Cain just said. I think Abel wants to understand, but Cain? No. No he doesn't. What can we do about that?"

Troubling words, and Adam could find no answer. He took his own head in his hands and shook it, almost willing the answer to come. When he looked again at Eve, he saw she was staring at him, perplexed. Never had she seen him this distraught. She began to regret her words and opened her mouth to tell him so, but the look in his eyes stopped her, and he stood to his feet.

"I'll go check on our sons. I think they're asleep. Tomorrow they'll find out they have a sister. I hope they will be pleased. But if not......." He shrugged and walked away, leaving Eve alone with her precious daughter.

CHAPTER 9

That daughter grew and thrived under Eve's watchful eye. "Someone just like me," she confided softly to Adam, who nodded in agreement and pleasure.

"Just think," he said as they gazed at her small sleeping form, "that's what you would have looked like if……"

"If I hadn't come another way," she laughed back.

Adam laughed too, then remembered again the wonder of his first glimpse of Eve when He had awakened Adam to present her to him. In spite of days of backbreaking work, of sweat on his face often, of relentless frustrations, he could never forget that, but with the memory would come again the sorrow and the knowledge of what he, what they, had lost.

There was no going back. He knew that. They knew that. But the knowledge did not take away the pain. "The

Tree of the Knowledge of Good and Evil," he thought bitterly. (Genesis 2:17)   Little had he known what that knowledge really meant for both of them. The knowledge, yes, but no power to withstand the forces that were aligned against them, with that knowledge. If only…………

He stopped the thought which came with pursuing recrimination, day after day. He knew all too well where that thought led. Guilt. Angry words of blame between them. Words that led nowhere. So he stifled them as often as he could. He was sure Eve felt the same.

Only rarely did they bring up the subject now, but sometimes when their sons quarreled or used harshly unforgiving words, he and Eve would look at each other in sorrow, their eyes mirroring the "What can we do?" thoughts that such exchanges brought.

Each day brought its own challenges of work to provide food for their growing family, and left little time to grieve over what they had lost. And with increasing regularity Eve found herself in the condition of having another child to bear. She sometimes remembered the talks with Him in the beautiful Garden, where He had pointed out certain leaves or fruits that would be helpful to them.

She remembered His words after their disobedience, words that she now understood all too well – "I will greatly multiply your sorrow and your conception." (Genesis

3:16) Greatly multiply! Well, it was happening, though with increasing understanding she was able to cope with the signs that accompanied that conception, as well as the birth pangs she had so dreaded that first time.

She often wondered what fruit, what leaf or berry it was that would make possible a lessening of conception, and one day she asked Adam about it.

"Yes, I remember He talked about things that would be good for us. But……"

He hesitated so long that Eve had to urge him on to finish his thought.

"But what? What are you trying to remember?"

"I……I think………"

"You think what? Tell me! Don't you remember anything?"

"I don't think we have those fruits now………… They were there, in the garden, but now, well, I………… they're gone."

"Why won't He let us have them?" The anger in her voice surprised Adam for a moment.

"They were part of ……….part of then. This is now."

Eve's anger faded quickly as she recognized the truth of Adam's words. "Then……….and now. It's no use. No way to go. Just……do what we've been doing. Be fruitful and multiply." (Genesis 1:28) Her words ended in a bit of a groan. Then she looked at Adam and began to laugh.

He was amazed, again, at how swiftly her moods could change. From anger, to …..this. This laughter. Inwardly he thought, "I'll never understand this woman that He gave me. Never!" and the thought made him smile.

Seeing him smile and join in her laughter lightened Eve's spirit and she forgot the frustration that had started her quest for knowledge of a fruit or a berry or a leaf to help her curb her childbearing. Looking over at their sons wrestling on the grass, she realized what a blessing they were. Beings like her and like Adam. Gifts – from Him.

CHAPTER 10

After that particular conversation Adam tried his best to remember His words in the Garden. The fruits He had pointed out to them. The berries and leaves. His words about how those fruits were good for them. As he went about his work he tried to find some of those, but to no avail. He too remembered those solemn words spoken to Eve: "I will greatly multiply your sorrow and your conception." (Genesis 3:16)

Greatly multiply? Well, He had told them to be fruitful. What did that mean? How many children would they have? Were they the only ones who were to multiply?

The thought had not come to him before, but now he began to wonder. When Cain and Abel grew older, would they too become fathers? How could that happen?

Adam stopped in his tracks. Eve had just produced a

being like herself. So – when that small one was grown, would she………………

"I've got to talk with Eve about this," he reasoned. "Of course, that's far in the future, but we'll have to talk about it anyway."

So that evening when their three were asleep, he brought up the subject.

"Have you ever thought about -- about our children having children?"

Her reply surprised him. "Yes."

"You have? Really?"

"You really think I'm the only one to ever have children in this whole place? I hope not."

His smile matched hers for a moment, but then he asked the question that had been bothering him. "Where will we find wives for our sons?"

Eve's smile broadened. "Where do you think? Right here! When this little one grows up, she will, -- well, she will be to Cain or Abel what I am to you, and together they will have children, just as you and I are doing!"

Adam nodded in agreement. "How else could it happen? We're the only ones here! Yes, I think you are correct. That's the way it will be!"

He thought about that conversation more and more as the days went by, days that saw their daughter grow well under Eve's careful nurturing. Adam admired her ways with their children. He was amazed sometimes at her perceptions. Still, it was difficult to listen to the discord that came between their children, difficult and disturbing.

Between him and Eve there had come a guarded carefulness in their interactions. They both realized how close to discord they often came, only to retreat from it in a mutual understanding that it would lead to no good.

Adam had continued keeping records of those first days in the Garden, of their talks with Him as they had walked together in the cool of the day. He tried hard to remember just what the words had been, about the creation of the world as they knew it, of the beautiful Garden where he and Eve had lived, of the animal friends they had. No discord there! How wonderful had been those days together, together with Him.

And now……….Now the best they could do were those times of offering sacrifices, of the chance of catching a glimpse of Him. As the days went on even with sacrifices offered time after time, those glimpses seemed to lessen, leaving Adam feeling empty and bereft.

He and Eve talked about their feelings now and then, but sometimes the sorrow and guilt were so overwhelming they had to stop. Sometimes she found him with the clay tablets, doing the keeping of records.

"Adam, why do you do that? What's the need?"

"I – Oh, I somehow think there is a need, somewhere. A need inside me to keep doing this, to remember what happened back there, in the Garden. To remember His words……"

"Why? What good does that do? It just ………… Oh, I don't know. We can't go back there, so why…………………….." Eve let the words trail off as she looked at the marks Adam was making with a sharp stick in the soft clay. "Well, tell me about this, then."

"See, here it is, the way He told us. 'In the beginning God created the heavens and the earth.' " (Genesis 1:1)

"Yes, I remember that. I remember Him telling us."

"He showed me how to make these marks when I named the animals."

"What was that like, finding names for them? Was it hard?"

Adam winced a bit at the word, recalling how Eve had used it in asking him about the process of having their first child. That seemed so long ago, but the memory was still fresh. Of course, now that Eve had borne three, she no longer asked him that difficult question, to which he had hardly known how to reply.

Now she knew full well what lay ahead when her body swelled like a ripe melon and when the pains began to come. Adam's record-keeping began to include days -- sunsets, sunrises, sunsets, sunrises. He well-remembered the words: "the evening and the morning were the first day," so he always started his calculations with the sunsets. (Genesis 1:5)   In all of those calculations, he had begun to be aware of the time intervals that were needed for yet another child to be born to them.

Would the next child be another son? Another daughter? He had no way of knowing, but again he remembered the words, "Be fruitful and multiply." (Genesis 1:28) He knew there would be more, unendingly.

Unendingly? Again, a stab of pain. No, there would be an end. Sometime. Where? When? That he did not know. He pushed the thought away. That would be – to die. He flinched from the word, even as he had to acknowledge it was true.

CHAPTER 11

True to the sunsets and sunrises, the days wore on, and on, and on. He tried to match his calculations of time with what he saw in the sky -- the stars, the moon, and their positions in the heavens, straining to remember His words about these wonders, about their creation.

Sometimes bone-weary at the close of another day of labor in the fields and with the animals, he could barely make himself attend to these matters, but something inside drove him to do it anyway.

Certainly their family was growing. Twelve more daughters. Eleven more sons. All needing care and tending – and food. "In the sweat of your face you shall eat bread." (Genesis 3:19) Often as he worked, the words would ring in his ears, even as he had heard them from Him.

With growth of the number of their family there came help with the work as Cain and Abel and the other sons grew older, and Adam admitted that that was good – good for him and for the work. The flocks and herds needed tending. Fences needed repairing. And weeds. Ah yes, the weeds.

"It wasn't that hard in the Garden," Adam would mutter to himself. "Here…….." and he let the thought carry him back to those days in the Garden, before…….. now. "He told us we should 'tend and keep' things there and we had it easy. (Genesis 2:15) I didn't know the meaning of 'hard,' – no, I didn't."

He did acknowledge over time that what he and Eve had talked about – it seemed so long ago now – was beginning to come to pass. Already some of their sons had begun their own families.

As he worked, he remembered the conversation he and Eve had had after a son had approached him. He told her what that particular son had said, about wanting to begin his own family.

"How are you going to do it?"

"How am I going to do what?" He hadn't expected such a question. .

"You can't just say -- 'Go' can you?"

"Why not? He has already built his own place, and……"

"What are you going to say?"

Adam's brow puckered in a frown. To himself, he said, "Will she never stop asking these questions? What does she mean, anyway?" Then aloud, "What should I say?"

Eve's answer was quick in coming, as if she had been thinking of this very thing for a long time. "What did He say to you?"

Caught off guard, Adam took a deep breath while he tried to remember. "Oh. I see what you mean. In the Garden."

"Where else?"

A sharp retort was on his lips, but he pressed them together, as he ran his fingers through his hair. He looked over at Eve who sat with her hands clasped together in front of her. No infant to feed for now. The pace of childbearing was slowing a bit.

"I remember when He brought you to me." The memory blotted out his feelings of exasperation that had tried to surface just now. "You were beautiful."

"Were?"

"You still are. My Eve."

"So what did He say when He brought me to you?"

"First, He said 'It isn't good that man should be alone,' (Genesis 2:18) so He made the animals and brought them to me, so I could find names for them. So

– I wasn't alone anymore."

"Yes, I know. Then what did He do?"

"You know the story."

"I want to hear it again."

"He put me into a deep sleep. Of course I don't remember that part. He told me later."

"And when you woke?"

"There you were! I said, 'This is now bone of my bones, and flesh of my flesh.' " (Genesis 2:23)

A frown flitted across Eve's face. Looking at her, Adam wondered what was wrong. Then she started to laugh. "Well, you can't say that to our son!"

Her mischievous laughter lifted the tension of the moment. "Can't say – what? Oh, 'Bone of my' ………. No, I won't be able to say that."

"I could say it, because I have carried our children inside me, but…."

"It's not the same. Not what He meant."

"Yes, I know! So what else is there?"

"He said, 'Therefore a man shall leave his father and mother and be joined to his wife, and they shall become one flesh." (Genesis 2:24)

"The way we have been. Of course, we didn't have a father and mother to leave, did we!" Eve sat weaving her fingers in and out.

"No, we didn't." Adam creased his brow into a frown

as he tried to remember what He had said back there in the Garden. "I do remember…. before all that, He said to me, 'It is not good for you to be alone.' (Genesis 2:18) Yes, I could tell that to our son."

"Yes, that will be a good thing to say. You can tell him He wanted me for you….."

"He did, yes, and it is a good thing."

"Even when it has ended like -- like this?"

The question pierced his heart with pain. They had left most of such talk well in the past. It was always there, of course, forming a background of who they were, but they rarely brought it up anymore.

All of this flashed through Adam's mind in a moment of time, but he knew he had to have an answer for Eve, who was looking at him, anticipating an answer – now! Not later. Now.

He spoke carefully, from his heart. "Yes, even now. A good thing. Always."

Eve stood, holding out her hand to Adam, who grasped it and stood beside her, then tenderly took her in his arms. She nestled there.

She remembered – oh so long ago now, -- how He had said, 'Your desire will be for your husband, and he shall rule over you.' and her heart acknowledged the truth of those words, as she whispered,"Yes, Adam. A good thing for me, too. Always." (Genesis 3:16)

CHAPTER 12

That was how it had begun, the "joining" ceremony that he and Eve used ever after. But Cain, having heard about Adam's conversation with one of his brothers, insisted that he be the first to choose a wife from among his sisters.

That brother agreed without anger, because the sister Cain chose, the second daughter Eve bore, was not the one he himself had decided upon. Adam and Eve were glad of the peaceful outcome of what could have been contentious. Cain had long since established himself as a leader not to be questioned, and the parents were glad these decisions did not cause a quarrel.

They had gone to the altar at the edge of the Garden, taking a lamb from the flock. Adam stood in front of the two of them, with Eve at his side, explaining to their children again about their beginnings. "He made me first, then the animals, and gave me the task of naming them all. He said it was not good for me to be alone." (Genesis 2:18)

Throughout the telling of this, Cain looked a bit bored, as though he had heard it all before, and of course, he had.

"Then," Adam recounted, "as good as all the animals were, there was really no one like myself. So He put me to sleep and from a bone in my side, He made – your mother! The mother of all living!" (Genesis 3:20)

His daughter listened carefully, her hand in Cain's. She too had heard the story many times from her mother, but she knew instinctively that this was an important day in which to hear it again.

Adam concluded, "It was not good for me to be alone, and it is not good for you two. So, 'Be fruitful and multiply!' (Genesis 1:28) That is what He said to me, and I am saying it to you both today. And I will sacrifice a lamb on the altar to show the importance of what you are doing."

Cain shrugged his shoulders, almost disdainfully, but offered no complaint. Afterwards, he took his new wife to the house he had built, for such a time as this.

Adam and Eve went back to their own house, Adam's mind full of questions. "Was that good enough, my Eve?"

"Yes, it was good. I'm not sure Cain was happy about it all, but it had to be done. It was important for you to say those words. They both needed to hear them."

"Cain didn't seem to like it that well. Almost as though he thought he had heard the words before."

"Of course he had. So had she. But they both needed to hear them again. This was a special day."

"I hope they both felt that."

"I think they did. And the time will come when they will have their own family."

Those words proved true. Soon Cain and his wife did have a child, and then more and more of Adam and Eve's children came to ask for the same ceremony which had joined Cain to his wife.

The time came when Eve found herself happily performing midwifery duties for her daughters. She told Adam, "I'm glad I can do this for them. After all, I had no one to help me."

Listening, Adam was annoyed. "Eve, wasn't I there for you? We talked about it, remember? And I tried……"

Eve's hand went to her mouth as she realized what she had said and how Adam was feeling about her words. "Yes, yes, my Adam, I know. You tried. We did it – together. But – I ……… as a woman, well ………..it's good to have someone who has gone through it herself…………"

Seeing her reaction, Adam smiled. "Well, yes, I see

what you mean. I know. There's something in a woman that needs another woman to ....understand." Then he added, "Even as between us men, we understand each other in a way that's different, too."

"Isn't that why He made us – different?"

"I'm sure it is. Even if we were still in the Garden, ...we'd be different from one another."

"Different but both created by Him. Aren't we doing what He wanted?"

"Of course we are. He said to be fruitful and multiply, and that's what's happening!" (Genesis 1:28)

Not long after that, Eve began another cycle of childbearing, five daughters, seven sons. She and Adam knew very well that they were fulfilling His words to them about being fruitful!

Abel had recently taken a wife from among his younger sisters, and they lived happily off in the distance in the house he had built near the animal pens Abel had constructed from stones. Definitely a shepherd, he loved to take good care of his sheep and lambs, and his wife, too, enjoyed helping him. Eve remembered how even as a little boy, the animals had been special to Abel, different from Cain's reaction, she acknowledged ruefully.

Abel was often faithful in bringing a sacrifice of one of his lambs to the altar at the edge of the Garden, taking his wife with him, both of them coming away each time with a sense that what they had done had pleased Him.

Both Adam and Eve were happy to see Abel content in his work, glad that he was careful to follow the teaching that Adam had tried to instill in all of their children. But one day something happened to upset the rhythm of their days. Something went terribly wrong.

CHAPTER 13

That particular day Abel had sacrificed a lamb as he often did. Adam had witnessed the sacrifice and was happy to catch a glimpse of Him, through the smoke of the sacrifice, and briefly saw a smile of approval. (Genesis 4:4)

Shortly after, Cain came to the altar and Adam was surprised to see in his arms not a lamb but an armful of produce from his garden. (Genesis 4:3) Adam knew how proud Cain was of his garden. He really enjoyed producing growing things.

"You always did like to help me when I worked in the garden," he told Cain, "but surely you know that what He really wants as a sacrifice is – a lamb!"

"Why? I think these things I've grown in my garden are every bit as good as those lambs that Abel raises!

Why shouldn't I bring these?"

"Because – Cain, -- I've told you, I've shown you, so many times, it's a lamb He wants. He killed a lamb to make clothing for your mother and me, that day when we disobeyed Him. It is only right that we do this to show we agree with Him and want to do this for Him."

"Well, I don't want to do that any more. I've been doing it, just as you said, but now I think what I have raised in my own garden is every bit as good as what Abel has in his sheep pens!"

"Cain, no, those things won't do!"

"I think they will do just fine. Besides, I'd have to barter with Abel for a lamb, and – I just don't want to do that today! I've been doing that – the bartering – long enough. I have my own household now and I should be able to do what I want!"

Foreboding grew in Adam's heart. He tried again. "Is it so hard to get a lamb from your brother? He has plenty of them and would be glad to get some of your produce in return!"

"Then let him grow the produce himself."

"No, I don't mean…………..No, Cain. It's just that what He really wants is a lamb."

"That's what you've always said. But today I want to bring – this," and he pointed to the produce he had placed upon the altar.

Troubled, Adam went back to the house. He shared his misgivings with Eve.

"Maybe this once He will take the produce, -- isn't that possible, Adam?"

"No, I don't think so. I have always known that a lamb is what He wants. It goes back to – you know, the day we disobeyed, and He killed a lamb to make coverings for us." (Genesis 3:21)

"But with Cain so sure that his garden stuff is good enough………"

"That's the trouble. I don't think it is good enough. Not really."

"What do you think will happen?"

"I -- I don't know. I hope…………..I hope nothing bad. It all makes me very afraid."

CHAPTER 14

Adam's fears seemed unnecessary by the next day. He purposefully visited the altar at the side of the Garden gate and saw the smoldering remains of the produce Cain had brought.

"Perhaps He did accept those things," Adam thought, gazing across to the other side of the Garden through the trees, straining his eyes to catch a glimpse of Him, but to no avail. "Through all this time, have I been mistaken?" The thought jarred him, as he went out to his own garden to work the soil again.

For another day his mind was unsettled, but then he made up his mind to let go of his concerns. "Surely it will be all right," he thought.

But soon a visit from Abel's wife unsettled him again. The sun was high in the sky when she came to their house. "Have you seen Abel today?" she asked, her voice concerned and shaky.

"No, no, I haven't," he answered. "Have you asked your mother?"

"Yes, and she hasn't seen him at all. He went to the sheep pens this morning and always comes for a mid-day meal but today he did not come."

"Have you looked………"

"Yes, everywhere. I went to the sheep pens. He's not there."

"Have you gone to any of the gardens?"

"No, because Abel doesn't spend much time there."

"Is he visiting at one of the other places, and forgot the time? He knows when the sun is high in the sky………."

She gazed at him rather reproachfully. "No, he doesn't forget. He always comes."

A sense of alarmed foreboding clutched at Adam's throat. "I – I'll come with you to look."

Together they walked past the Garden gate, past the altar with its burden of charred vegetables. A distance away Adam saw birds circling low in the sky. The sight stirred unfamiliar fear in his heart. "Go back to your mother. I'll go see what those birds are doing."

Abel's wife hesitated, then turned back doubtfully.

"I'll just look over there, and come back soon." His feet felt heavy as he made his way toward the place where the birds were circling. What did he expect to find? A sense of dread built in his heart. He knew from experience why certain birds often gathered in places where an animal had died. Surely………. Should he call to Abel? When Abel was a small boy, they sometimes made a game of calling to one another. But today Abel's disappearance was very strange.

As he came closer to the place where the birds were circling, Adam saw someone lying in the grass. Lying very still. Was it Abel? Surely he wouldn't be sleeping out here! His mind whirled in disbelief. He approached the spot, then fell to his knees beside the still form of his son, Abel, whose head was terribly bloody and bruised, his eyes open, unseeing.

His heart pounded heavily and he cried out "Abel! Abel! Wake up! Wake up!" Tears of grief flooded his own eyes.

He heard footsteps behind him. Looking up, he saw Cain approach and heard his voice: "You've found him, then."

"Cain, what happened?"

"I was angry."

"What happened?"

"I – I did the sacrifice."

"The garden produce?" The question was unnecessary. He knew the answer.

"Yes. The way I said I would. And He – He did not like what I brought."

"How do you know?"

"He told me. He said Abel's offering was better."

"Cain, isn't that what I – "

"He asked me why I was angry. Didn't He already know?"

"What else did He say?"

"He asked me, 'If you do well, won't you be accepted? And if you don't do well, sin lies at the door.' (Genesis 4:7) And yes, I was angry."

"So – you did this? To your own brother?"

"Why are you asking me? Already He has asked me that!"

"What did He say?"

"He said, 'Where is Abel your brother?' and I said, 'I don't know. Am I my brother's keeper?'" (Genesis 4:9)

"But – you did know!"

"Yes, I did know. And He did, too. I didn't know He would see. He said, 'What have you done? The voice of your brother's blood cries to me from the ground.' (Genesis 4:10) I didn't know that He could hear -- that."

"What else did He say then?"

For the first time, Cain's voice broke with emotion. "He said I am cursed from the earth that has taken my brother's blood. He said when I try to grow things, they won't grow for me anymore. He said I'll be a fugitive and a vagabond in the earth." (Genesis 4:11-12)

"How did you answer him?"

"What could I say? I told him the bitter truth. I said, 'My punishment is greater than I can bear.'" (Genesis 4:13)

"You said that? – to Him?"

"Yes, and I told Him, "You are driving me out today from the face of the ground; I shall be hidden from Your face; I shall be a fugitive and a vagabond on the earth, and it will happen that anyone who finds me will kill me." (Genesis 4: 14)

"Cain, Cain, I can hardly believe this has happened. It's terrible…….."

Cain kept his face averted from his father, ignoring his words, and a touch of wonder was in his voice as his next words came: "He told me that whoever kills me will get vengeance seven times over! Seven times!" (Genesis 4:15)

Adam had started to rise to his feet at Cain's words, and Cain suddenly looked at his father, with both hands outstretched to help Adam get up. Adam gasped. On Cain's forehead was the picture of a lamb. On Cain's right hand, the same picture of a lamb.

"This – this is on my hand now."

Adam's words came slowly, "And on your forehead."

Cain put his left hand to his head. "Here?"

"Yes, Cain, there. What did He say about that?"

"He told me He was putting a mark upon me so that no one who found me would kill me. (Genesis 4:15) It's as if "--- here the tone of wonder came back into Cain's voice, "as if He actually values my life................" His words trailed off and he shook his head as if to clear away the confusion and disbelief that had drifted in.

In his own confusion and sorrow Adam did not know how to answer his son. All his life he had been telling Cain about Him. What had he missed in the telling? Something. Because Cain had never seemed to feel the connection, the caring that he was giving evidence of just now. Words failed Adam.

But Cain continued. "He put this mark on me so that no one who found me would kill me. (Genesis 4:15) I thought it was only on my hand. A lamb. The mark of – what I did not want to give Him." Here his voice broke. "And when others see it, they will know too."

"What will they know? I don't understand."

"They'll know He put the mark on me because I didn't want to give – what I should have given. I was to give a lamb. They'll know He put this mark on me and when they see it, they'll know He wants me to live. Live with the knowledge that I was wrong."

"Will that make a difference to them?"

"I hope so. It makes a difference to me – now!"

"Where – where will you go?" Adam's question came out of despair.

"I – I have to go somewhere, somewhere out there," and he jerked his head quickly to the left. "That's what He said. I'll be a – a wanderer."

"Have you told – your wife?"

"Not yet. I'll have to explain the mark. She'll come with me, I'm sure."

"A wanderer! Do – do you really want that?"

Cain's voice was harsh. "Want that? No, never. All I have ever wanted is to be – to have what I have here, making things grow. I've always loved that. You know…."

"Yes, I know very well how you've always loved to be in the fields, growing things. Even when you were small, you liked to follow me……"

"I think He knows that. That's why the punishment of being a wanderer is so hard. But it's the way He got my attention. At last."

Adam sank to his knees with a low moan. He turned his head again and looked at the body of Abel, lying so still beside him. "We – we'll have to do something about – this."

"Should we tell -- her?"

Adam's heart raced. In the horror of the past few

moments, he had not once thought of Eve, and of Abel's wife. Now he knew he could no longer delay in letting them know what had happened to Abel. "Yes, I – we must tell her, and Abel's wife. I -- this is hard, but it must be done."

Hard. That word again. New meanings that he had never imagined before when he used the word. Something hard that must be done.

CHAPTER 15

It was hard, harder than he had thought possible. Eve was inconsolable. He had never seen her so distraught. And Abel's wife, their daughter, was speechless with shock and sorrow. At first Adam was sorry that he had brought them to the place so they could see Abel for themselves, but later he knew that that was the only thing he could have done.

Cain was not there when they reached Abel's body. Adam wondered vaguely where he had gone. The question "Has he left already?" raced through his mind, though he did not voice his concern.

Eve's voice was a loud lament as she kneeled beside her son. "Abel, Abel, come back! Come back!" Her cries echoed across the fields.

Abel's wife kneeled with tears streaming down her

face. As she lifted her head she saw Cain coming in the distance, a digging tool in his grip, and she rose, wringing her hands in despair. "I can't – I don't want to see him just now," she gasped, then added, "I'm going to go see – my sister…" and she began to run across the fields toward Cain's house.

Cain kept his head down as he came near where Adam and Eve kneeled beside Abel's body. Adam had not yet told Eve about the mark. Time for that later, he thought briefly.

His thoughts were interrupted by a scream from Eve. "Cain, look at me! What have you done! How could you……." and her words ended in a sob. She stood beside her first-born, hands covering her eyes. Then she lifted her hands to cradle Cain's face.

His face wore an expression she had not seen there before. Gone was his usual assured self-confidence, replaced by a mixture of grief, resignation, despair and something else she did not understand.

Her eyes took in all of that, then the mark on his forehead. "Cain, what -- what is this -- this mark? (Genesis 4:15) It looks like a lamb! When…….."

"He put it there!"

Eve's eyes searched Adam's as he stood beside her. "You?……"

"No, no, He did it. Cain told me."

Cain held out his right hand. "Here, too."

"He? Oh, -- yes, I -- but what does it mean?" Eve's voice was still full of tears.

"It's -- so no-one will kill me, the way I killed – him." And Cain's head inclined toward the still figure on the ground. "See, it's on my hand as well."

Eve searched his eyes, then took Cain's right hand in her own, looking in wonder at the image of a lamb etched there. "He put it there? What did He tell you?"

"It's -- yes, He put it there. When I see it, I'll be reminded of what I've done. Of what I should have done. All that."

"All that." Eve's words echoed the thought. "I can't believe………"

"Believe. It's done. I'll – I'll pay forever." Eve's heart wrenched at the bitterness in Cain's tone. "Others will see what's on my – my head, and I'll see it on my hand so I'll never forget."

"Forget? How can we forget!" Eve's voice was sharp with disbelief.

"No, we can't. We won't. I -- I'll be going away. Away from all of this," and his left arm made a circle in the air, pointing to the well-tended fields.

"But – why?" Eve's voice was still distraught.

"Didn't he tell you?" and his eyes questioned Adam.

"No, no, I didn't tell her – yet."

"Tell me what?" Eve's hands were twisting together, a mirror of her swirling thoughts.

"You tell her, Cain. Tell her what you told me."

"He said – because of what I have done, the earth has taken my – my brother's blood and now, that earth will not -- I will not be able to grow things anymore and -- I'll be a wanderer on the face of the earth." (Genesis 4:11-12) Cain's words came haltingly as he tried to explain to Eve what his punishment would be.

She listened in horror. "But Cain, you've always loved to grow things….."

"I know. I know. But – no more. No more."

"A wanderer? What does that mean? Where will you go? How – how will you live?"

Cain shook his head. "I – I don't know. I haven't figured that out yet."

"Will – will your wife go too?"

"Yes, I think so. She saw the mark so I had to tell her – about how I got it, and why."

"What did she say?" Eve's heart was heavy as she thought about her daughter's life and what this could mean for all of them.

"She – she just looked at me and then she started to cry. That's when I went to get this digging stick………" Cain's voice trailed off and he took a deep breath as if to clear his head.

"Digging – yes, yes, we'll need to – to do that for –" Adam's voice broke; "for Abel's body. We can't just – leave him here," and his eyes took in the large birds circling in the blue sky above them.

Eve cringed. "You mean – put him there, in the ground?"

"We can't just leave him here." Adam repeated again what he had said only moments before.

Eve fell to the ground again, beside Abel's body. "My son! Come back! If only….." Her voice broke into sobs again. She touched his hands, feeling the coldness that had come into them, and she drew back in horror.

Adam stooped to raise her up from the ground, saying gently, "Cain and I will do this. Go back to the house."

Nodding mutely, Eve rose and turned to go. Cain avoided her eyes and turned to start probing the earth in front of him with his digging stick.

Adam's arm pointed to the edge of the field where there were trees. "Let's dig over there, Cain," he murmured tonelessly, all the while keeping his eyes on Eve's departing form, seeing her slumped shoulders still shaking with sobs. Without a word Cain nodded and together they headed for the trees.

So within the trees' welcoming shelter they dug a shallow grave into which they put Abel's cold lifeless body. All the while Adam's thoughts swirled relentlessly.

He was sure he would awaken soon and find this had been an awful dream. In the midst of all the chaos, he could not imagine what Cain was thinking.

Cain's face was stony and he kept his thoughts to himself. When they had finished putting the earth on top of Abel's body, he looked up at the sky where the birds were no longer circling.

Numbly Adam's eyes too searched the sky. He looked past the trees and saw a few animals lurking there. "Cain, we'd better get some stones to put on top of this – this earth," and silently Cain nodded and began to gather some of the larger ones nearby. His muscular arms carried them easily, and together they piled them carefully over the fresh dirt under which Abel's body lay.

The sun was low in the sky by the time they had finished. "I'll be going back now, to – to my house." Cain's words jolted Adam, as he realized that probably it would be for the last time. Where would Cain again find a permanent place to rest? A wanderer! What would that really mean for Cain, for his wife, for their children? He did not know.

"Yes," was all Adam could manage, as he turned to go home to Eve.

CHAPTER 16

Days later he and Eve stood beside the pile of stones that marked Abel's grave. Eve stood with tears running down her cheeks, sobs catching in her throat. She turned to Adam for comfort, and he gathered her in his arms.

Only then did she voice a concern that had been bothering her. "What – what will happen to – Abel's body?" There, it was out, a worry that had cut deep.

The question did not surprise Adam, for he had been thinking about that too, and had reached some conclusions. "It'll just – go back to – to dust." (Genesis 3:19)

"But why?" Eve twisted around quickly to look into Adam's face. "No! That can't be – how can that be so?"

Her reaction was so frantic and startled that for a long moment Adam didn't know how to answer. Then carefully he phrased his own question: "How can it not be so?"

"Because – because it's my son! He is – was – precious! How can he just turn back into dust? That's not fair. How do you know that, -- how?"

"I know that because He said it. Don't you remember His words?" (Genesis 3:19)

"I don't think I want to remember, if that's what He said."

"Even so, He did say it. I've kept a record on those clay tablets, when I'd sit and try to remember what He said to us in the Garden."

Eve slumped down onto one of the larger stones on Abel's mound. She took a deep breath, then said wistfully, "I wish you hadn't remembered."

"No, it's good that I did. Because now we know – what will happen."

"I don't like it."

Adam's voice was grim. "And I don't – like it, either, Eve. But that doesn't keep it from being true."

"All right. Tell me just what He said. Maybe hearing it, I will remember too."

"We didn't really understand when He said the words, -- how could we, just then? but He put it like this: 'In the sweat of your face you shall eat bread till you return to the ground. For out of it you were taken, For dust you are, and to dust you shall return.' " (Genesis 3:19)

Eve shivered. "Yes, I – I think I do remember now.

And no, we didn't really understand then, any more than we can now."

Adam chose another of the stones and sat down beside Eve. "One of the reasons we put these stones here is so that – no animal can dig it up and -- "

"Oh, Adam, don't say it! Better to have his body stay here and go back to dust than – than that!" Eve's voice was shrill, and tears were ready to fall again.

For a brief moment Adam wished he had not brought up the reason for the stones, but the words were out, the damage done. He sighed heavily. "I shouldn't have told you about the stones……"

"Yes, yes, you should have. I did wonder. I thought, 'Why stones? They look so ugly! Why not just the green grass?' "

"That's the reason, so, now you know."

"Did Cain help put them here?"

"Yes, yes he did. His arms are strong. He lifts well."

"He worked hard in the fields, Adam. I wonder where he and – our daughter are now, and their children."

"They went to the East of the Garden, when they left." (Genesis 4:16)

"Will we ever see them again? Will they – wander – this way again?"

"I don't know. He didn't say."

"I'm glad Abel's wife gave them those sheepskins

Abel had in their house. She told me she gave them to her sister."

"Was Cain happy about that?"

"I don't know, but I think he will be when he finds out they need some kind of shelter and there's no house to stay in."

"Was that Abel's idea?"

"I think so. Our daughter said he had made a nice shelter for some of his lambs, using sheepskins and tree branches. If they have to be wanderers……….." Eve left her thought unfinished and stood, shivering, wrapping her arms around herself.

Adam stood too, then mused in an awestruck tone, "Just think. Cain taking shelter under lambskins!"

"Oh, Adam, do you think he will remember why he has the mark of a lamb on his head and hand now?"

Adam tried to make his voice sound more confident than he felt. "How can he forget? Of course, he'll remember. He'll see the mark on his right hand, and he'll know that everyone else will see it on his forehead. He'll remember that He put the mark on him so that others won't – won't do to him what he did to – his brother." Adam's voice broke.

Eve looked up at Adam, surprised by his tone and his emotion. "Come, let's go back to our house. We've been here long enough."

CHAPTER 17

It had not taken long for the news about Cain and Abel to spread, and everyone knew that Cain and his wife had gone away, to be wanderers in the earth. They knew about the mark and why it had been given to Cain.

Each time Adam and Eve sacrificed a lamb on the altar at the side of the Garden, their thoughts went to their firstborn and they wondered about him and his family.

Soon Eve again found herself in the now-familiar process of bearing another child. To Adam she said, "Perhaps this will be another son."

Adam remembered well her belief that Abel would be a son, and that had proved true. "You think this will be a son, then?"

"Yes, I think so."

When the time came for the birth, Eve's words proved

true. "We'll call him Seth," she said with certainty, "because God has given me another to take the place of Abel, whom Cain killed." (Genesis 4:25)

Adam nodded in agreement. He added Eve's words to his account that he had been keeping on the clay tablets. The tablets were many now, and he treasured them, keeping them in a safe place inside their house.

Those tablets recorded many, many sunsets and sunrises. Together Adam and Eve lived them, worked through them, worked through their sorrow at the loss of their sons, their first-born as well as his brother. One buried in the earth not far away. The other gone very far away to wander the earth. Both gone, never to return to Adam and Eve.

Eve treasured Seth in a special way, since for her he had taken Abel's place. As he grew, she often tried to tell him about the children she had had before, and about the Garden where she and Adam had lived.

A long time later, after Seth had grown and had taken a wife, Seth had a son whom he named Enosh and Eve was happy beyond words to watch the growth of this young son.

The time she spent with Enosh reminded her of the early days she and Adam had had with Cain and Abel. She delighted in telling Enosh of those days.

She repeated the stories often to Enosh, and as he

grew, Eve found him asking questions about "those times."

"Eema Eve, tell me again about when my father was born," he would beg.

"Enosh, that was a – a happy day, when your father came into our lives. You see, he took the place of another son whom we loved dearly."

"What was his name?"

"His name was Abel."

"Where is he now?"

The question never got easier for Eve to answer. Always there was the catch in her throat, the sharp pain in her heart as she remembered Abel. "He -- Well, come, Enosh, we can go to see the place where we put him into the ground."

Over time Enosh knew the place well. Now the stones were overgrown with grass, but Eve tried to keep it trimmed and neat. The task gave her a feeling of comfort. She and Enosh would go there, and stand while Eve related the story he came to know almost as well as she did.

"Then Cain, Abel's brother, hit him so he died?"

"Yes, Abel died. His blood went into the ground. Then He told Cain that he had done wrong and must leave this place and be a wanderer."

"This One who told Cain that – He knew about it

even though Cain didn't think anyone saw what he did?"

"Yes, He knew."

"He must be very wise, that One."

"Oh, yes, Enosh, He was very wise. He is the One who made Adam and me and put us into that beautiful Garden. We lived there and it was a wonderful place."

"But you had to leave it."

Eve saw that Enosh had faithfully remembered the words she had been telling him so often. "Yes, we did not obey what He told us, and……"

"Why didn't you obey? Didn't you believe Him? Didn't you know how wise He really was?"

Eve smiled to herself, marveling at this young one's questions. "He reminds me of Abel, the way he understands so much," she said to herself.

Out loud she answered, "We knew He was wise but a serpent came and tricked me. He told me that if I ate the fruit we had been told not to eat, then I would be as wise as that One is, and I thought that would be a good thing." (Genesis 3:4-5)

"And it would have been good, wouldn't it?"

"Well, maybe, and perhaps the day would have come when He would have let us eat it after all. I don't know. But we jumped ahead of that and did not obey."

"So He told you to leave the beautiful Garden?"

"Yes, and we could never go back."

"Did you try?"

"It was no use. There were some angels there and a flaming sword to keep us from going back. So we knew we could never be there anymore."

"So that's when you made this?"

By now they had walked back to where the altar stood in what had been a corner of the Garden. "Yes, we felt closer to Him when we would sacrifice a lamb here. Sometimes we would see Him through the trees over there, behind the altar, and we knew He was pleased."

Enosh was quiet for a moment. "I'd like to see Him, Eema Eve," he said softly.

Eve caught her breath. He sounded so wistful. Again she was reminded of Abel. "Tell your father you want to bring a lamb to sacrifice soon."

"The way Abel did?"

"Yes, that way."

"I'll ask my father. And I think there will be others who might want to do that, too, Eema Eve."

And there were. Enosh was convincing and joyful in telling others about that altar, the place of sacrifice.

Thus it was that in those days men began to call upon the name of the Lord. (Genesis 4:26)

THE END

Genesis 1

The History of Creation

1 In the beginning God created the heavens and the earth. 2 The earth was without form, and void; and darkness was on the face of the deep. And the Spirit of God was hovering over the face of the waters.
3 Then God said, "Let there be light"; and there was light. 4 And God saw the light, that it was good; and God divided the light from the darkness. 5 God called the light Day, and the darkness He called Night. So the evening and the morning were the first day.
6 Then God said, "Let there be a firmament in the midst of the waters, and let it divide the waters from the waters." 7 Thus God made the firmament, and divided the waters which were under the firmament from the waters which were above the firmament; and it was so. 8 And God called the firmament Heaven. So the evening and the morning were the second day.
9 Then God said, "Let the waters under the heavens be gathered together into one place, and let the dry land appear"; and it was so. 10 And God called the dry land Earth, and the gathering together of the waters He called Seas. And God saw that it was good.
11 Then God said, "Let the earth bring forth grass, the herb that yields seed, and the fruit tree that yields fruit according to its kind, whose seed is in itself, on the earth"; and it was so. 12 And the earth brought forth grass, the herb that yields seed according to its kind, and the tree that yields fruit, whose seed is in itself according to its kind. And God saw that it was good. 13 So the evening and the morning were the third day.
14 Then God said, "Let there be lights in the firmament of the heavens to divide the day from the night; and let them be for signs and seasons, and for days and years; 15 and let them be for lights in the firmament of the heavens to give light on the earth"; and it was so. 16 Then God made two great lights: the greater light to rule the day, and the lesser light to rule the night. He made the stars also. 17 God set them in the firmament of the heavens to give light on the earth, 18 and to rule over the day and over the night, and to divide the light from the darkness. And God saw that it

was good. 19 So the evening and the morning were the fourth day.

20 Then God said, "Let the waters abound with an abundance of living creatures, and let birds fly above the earth across the face of the firmament of the heavens." 21 So God created great sea creatures and every living thing that moves, with which the waters abounded, according to their kind, and every winged bird according to its kind. And God saw that it was good. 22 And God blessed them, saying, "Be fruitful and multiply, and fill the waters in the seas, and let birds multiply on the earth." 23 So the evening and the morning were the fifth day.

24 Then God said, "Let the earth bring forth the living creature according to its kind: cattle and creeping thing and beast of the earth, each according to its kind"; and it was so. 25 And God made the beast of the earth according to its kind, cattle according to its kind, and everything that creeps on the earth according to its kind. And God saw that it was good.

26 Then God said, "Let Us make man in Our image, according to Our likeness; let them have dominion over the fish of the sea, over the birds of the air, and over the cattle, over all the earth and over every creeping thing that creeps on the earth." 27 So God created man in His own image; in the image of God He created him; male and female He created them. 28 Then God blessed them, and God said to them, "Be fruitful and multiply; fill the earth and subdue it; have dominion over the fish of the sea, over the birds of the air, and over every living thing that moves on the earth."

29 And God said, "See, I have given you every herb that yields seed which is on the face of all the earth, and every tree whose fruit yields seed; to you it shall be for food. 30 Also, to every beast of the earth, to every bird of the air, and to everything that creeps on the earth, in which there is life, I have given every green herb for food"; and it was so. 31 Then God saw everything that He had made, and indeed it was very good. So the evening and the morning were the sixth day.

Genesis 2

1 Thus the heavens and the earth, and all the host of them, were finished. 2 And on the seventh day God ended His work which He had done, and He rested on the seventh day from all His work which He had done. 3 Then God blessed the seventh day and sanctified it, because in it He rested from all His work which God had created and made.

4 This is the history of the heavens and the earth when they were created, in the day that the LORD God made the earth and the heavens, 5 before any plant of the field was in the earth and before any herb of the field had grown. For the LORD God had not caused it to rain on the earth, and there was no man to till the ground; 6 but a mist went up from the earth and watered the whole face of the ground.

7 And the LORD God formed man of the dust of the ground, and breathed into his nostrils the breath of life; and man became a living being.

Life in God's Garden

8 The LORD God planted a garden eastward in Eden, and there He put the man whom He had formed. 9 And out of the ground the LORD God made every tree grow that is pleasant to the sight and good for food. The tree of life was also in the midst of the garden, and the tree of the knowledge of good and evil.

10 Now a river went out of Eden to water the garden, and from there it parted and became four riverheads. 11 The name of the first is Pishon; it is the one which skirts the whole land of Havilah, where there is gold. 12 And the gold of that land is good. Bdellium and the onyx stone are there. 13 The name of the second river is Gihon; it is the one which goes around the whole land of Cush. 14 The name of the third river is Hiddekel; it is the one which goes toward the east of Assyria. The fourth river is the Euphrates.

15 Then the LORD God took the man and put him in the garden of Eden to tend and keep it. 16 And the LORD God commanded the man, saying, "Of every tree of the garden you may freely eat; 17 but of the tree of the knowledge of good and evil you shall not eat,

for in the day that you eat of it you shall surely die."

18 And the LORD God said, "It is not good that man should be alone; I will make him a helper comparable to him." 19 Out of the ground the LORD God formed every beast of the field and every bird of the air, and brought them to Adam to see what he would call them. And whatever Adam called each living creature, that was its name. 20 So Adam gave names to all cattle, to the birds of the air, and to every beast of the field. But for Adam there was not found a helper comparable to him.

21 And the LORD God caused a deep sleep to fall on Adam, and he slept; and He took one of his ribs, and closed up the flesh in its place. 22 Then the rib which the LORD God had taken from man He made into a woman, and He brought her to the man.

23 And Adam said:

"This is now bone of my bones
And flesh of my flesh;
She shall be called Woman,

Because she was taken out of Man."

24 Therefore a man shall leave his father and mother and be joined to his wife, and they shall become one flesh.

25 And they were both naked, the man and his wife, and were not ashamed.

Genesis 3

The Temptation and Fall of Man

1 Now the serpent was more cunning than any beast of the field which the LORD God had made. And he said to the woman, "Has God indeed said, 'You shall not eat of every tree of the garden'?"
2 And the woman said to the serpent, "We may eat the fruit of the trees of the garden; 3 but of the fruit of the tree which is in the midst of the garden, God has said, 'You shall not eat it, nor shall you touch it, lest you die.'"
4 Then the serpent said to the woman, "You will not surely die. 5 For God knows that in the day you eat of it your eyes will be opened, and you will be like God, knowing good and evil."
6 So when the woman saw that the tree was good for food, that it was pleasant to the eyes, and a tree desirable to make one wise, she took of its fruit and ate. She also gave to her husband with her, and he ate. 7 Then the eyes of both of them were opened, and they knew that they were naked; and they sewed fig leaves together and made themselves coverings.
8 And they heard the sound of the LORD God walking in the garden in the cool of the day, and Adam and his wife hid themselves from the presence of the LORD God among the trees of the garden.
9 Then the LORD God called to Adam and said to him, "Where are you?"
10 So he said, "I heard Your voice in the garden, and I was afraid because I was naked; and I hid myself."
11 And He said, "Who told you that you were naked? Have you eaten from the tree of which I commanded you that you should not eat?"
12 Then the man said, "The woman whom You gave to be with me, she gave me of the tree, and I ate."
13 And the LORD God said to the woman, "What is this you have done?"
The woman said, "The serpent deceived me, and I ate."
14 So the LORD God said to the serpent:

"Because you have done this,
You are cursed more than all cattle,
And more than every beast

of the field;
On your belly you shall go,
And you shall eat dust
All the days of your life.
15 And I will put enmity
Between you and the woman,
And between your seed and
her Seed;
He shall bruise your head,
And you shall bruise His
heel."
16 To the woman He said:
"I will greatly multiply
your sorrow and
your conception;
In pain you shall bring
forth children;
Your desire shall be for your
husband,
And he shall rule over you."
17 Then to Adam He said,
"Because you have heeded the
voice of your wife, and have
eaten from the tree of which I
commanded you, saying, 'You
shall not eat of it':

"Cursed is the ground for
your sake;
In toil you shall eat of it
All the days of your life.

18 Both thorns and thistles it
shall bring forth for you,
And you shall eat the herb of
the field.

19 In the sweat of your face
you shall eat bread
Till you return to the ground,
For out of it you were taken;
For dust you are,
And to dust you shall return."
20 And Adam called his wife's name Eve, because she was the mother of all living.
21 Also for Adam and his wife the LORD God made tunics of skin, and clothed them.
22 Then the LORD God said, "Behold, the man has become like one of Us, to know good and evil. And now, lest he put out his hand and take also of the tree of life, and eat, and live forever"— 23 therefore the LORD God sent him out of the garden of Eden to till the ground from which he was taken. 24 So He drove out the man; and He placed cherubim at the east of the garden of Eden, and a flaming sword which turned every way, to guard the way to the tree of life.

Genesis 4

Cain Murders Abel

1 Now Adam knew Eve his wife, and she conceived and bore Cain, and said, "I have acquired a man from the LORD." 2 Then she bore again, this time his brother Abel. Now Abel was a keeper of sheep, but Cain was a tiller of the ground. 3 And in the process of time it came to pass that Cain brought an offering of the fruit of the ground to the LORD. 4 Abel also brought of the firstborn of his flock and of their fat. And the LORD respected Abel and his offering, 5 but He did not respect Cain and his offering. And Cain was very angry, and his countenance fell.
6 So the LORD said to Cain, "Why are you angry? And why has your countenance fallen? 7 If you do well, will you not be accepted? And if you do not do well, sin lies at the door. And its desire is for you, but you should rule over it."
8 Now Cain talked with Abel his brother; and it came to pass, when they were in the field, that Cain rose up against Abel his brother and killed him.
9 Then the LORD said to Cain, "Where is Abel your brother?" He said, "I do not know. Am I my brother's keeper?"
10 And He said, "What have you done? The voice of your brother's blood cries out to Me from the ground. 11 So now you are cursed from the earth, which has opened its mouth to receive your brother's blood from your hand. 12 When you till the ground, it shall no longer yield its strength to you. A fugitive and a vagabond you shall be on the earth."
13 And Cain said to the LORD, "My punishment is greater than I can bear! 14 Surely You have driven me out this day from the face of the ground; I shall be hidden from Your face; I shall be a fugitive and a vagabond on the earth, and it will happen that anyone who finds me will kill me."
15 And the LORD said to him, "Therefore, whoever kills Cain, vengeance shall be taken on him sevenfold." And the LORD set a mark on Cain, lest anyone finding him should kill him.

The Family of Cain

16 Then Cain went out from the presence of the LORD and dwelt in the land of Nod on the

east of Eden. 17 And Cain knew his wife, and she conceived and bore Enoch. And he built a city, and called the name of the city after the name of his son—Enoch. 18 To Enoch was born Irad; and Irad begot Mehujael, and Mehujael begot Methushael, and Methushael begot Lamech.

19 Then Lamech took for himself two wives: the name of one was Adah, and the name of the second was Zillah. 20 And Adah bore Jabal. He was the father of those who dwell in tents and have livestock. 21 His brother's name was Jubal. He was the father of all those who play the harp and flute. 22 And as for Zillah, she also bore Tubal-Cain, an instructor of every craftsman in bronze and iron. And the sister of Tubal-Cain was Naamah.

23 Then Lamech said to his wives:

"Adah and Zillah, hear my voice;
Wives of Lamech, listen to my speech!
For I have killed a man for wounding me,
Even a young man for hurting me.
  24 If Cain shall be avenged sevenfold,
Then Lamech seventy-sevenfold."

A New Son

25 And Adam knew his wife again, and she bore a son and named him Seth, "For God has appointed another seed for me instead of Abel, whom Cain killed." 26 And as for Seth, to him also a son was born; and he named him Enosh. Then men began to call on the name of the LORD.

CPSIA information can be obtained at www.ICGtesting.com
Printed in the USA
LVOW081338091011

249732LV00001B/3/P